This book is dedicated to my parents, brother, wife, nine children, and our cat.
- S.S

Text and illustrations copyright © 2007 by East West Discovery Press
Arabic translation copyright © 2008 by East West Discovery Press

Published by:
East West Discovery Press
P.O. Box 3585, Manhattan Beach, CA 90266
Phone: 310-545-3730, Fax: 310-545-3731
Website: www.eastwestdiscovery.com

Written and illustrated by Sunny Seki
Arabic translation by Translations.com
Arabic proofreading by Ray Saeid
Edited by Marcie Rouman
Book production by Luzelena Rodriguez
Production management by Icy Smith

ISBN-13: 978-0-9799339-3-6 Hardcover
Library of Congress Control Number: 2007937880
First Bilingual English and Arabic Edition 2008
Printed in China
Published in the United States of America

The Tale of the Lucky Cat is also available in English only and eight bilingual editions including English with Arabic, Chinese, Hmong, Japanese, Korean, Spanish, Tagalog and Vietnamese.

Japanese Glossary مسرد بالكلمات اليابانية :
Tama (تاما)/ شيء مستدير :*A round object*
Sensei(سنسي): كلمة تبجيل للمعلم / *A respectful word for teacher*
Osho (أوشو): زعيم معبد بوذي / *Leader of a Buddhist temple*
Osho-san(أوشو سان): *The respectful and friendly way to address the osho*/
osho الطريقة المتسمة بالاحترام والودودة لمخاطبة
Kokoro (كوكورو): *The mind or spirit of a living thing* / عقل أو روح كائن حي
Maneki (مانيكي): *Inviting or beckoning* / دعوة أو تلويح
Neko(نيكو)/ قطة: *Cat*

A long time ago in Japan, there lived a toymaker named Tokuzo. He was a kind young man who traveled from village to village to sell his toys at festivals.

يحكى أنه منذ زمن بعيد في اليابان، كان يعيش صانع ألعاب اسمه توكوزو. وكان توكوزو شاباً لطيفاً يسافر من قرية إلى أخرى لبيع ألعابه في المهرجانات.

Children liked his toys. Still, Tokuzo was making barely enough money to survive. "Someday," he thought, "I'll create something so unique that everyone will want to have it."

وكان الأطفال يحبون ألعابه. إلا أن توكوزو كان يكسب ما يكفيه للعيش بالكاد. "وذات يوم"، فكر قائلا، "سوف أصنع شيئاً ما فريداً للغاية بحيث سيرغب كل شخص في اقتنائه".

4

The next festival was big, and Tokuzo knew that he would be able to sell a lot of toys there. So he was in a hurry to get the best place. He started on his journey, but had no idea that soon his life was about to change.

وكان المهرجان التالي كبيراً، وكان توكوزو يعرف أنه سيتمكن من بيع عدد كبير من الألعاب فيه. ولذا كان متعجلاً للحصول على أفضل موقع ممكن. وبدأ رحلته، لكنه لم يكن يدري أن حياته سوف تتغير قريباً.

He had just entered a small village, when suddenly a frightened cat darted past him. It was being chased by a growling dog.

"Oh, no! Stop!" Tokuzo screamed because he saw an express-delivery horse speeding in their direction. He stood helplessly as the horse hit the cat.

دخل توكوزو لتوه إلى قرية صغيرة، عندما عبرت أمامه فجأة قطة خائفة يطاردها كلب ينبح.

وصرخ توكوزو أوه، كلا! توقف! لأنه رأى حصان بريد يتجه مسرعاً في اتجاههما. ووقف عاجزاً وهو يرى الحصان يصدم القطة.

7

The accident happened so quickly that the townspeople did not notice the cat at all. But Tokuzo saw that it had been badly hurt.

"Maybe I can save it. It's still breathing," he said. He quickly found an inn, and carried the cat inside.

لقد وقع الحادث بسرعة
خاطفة لدرجة أن سكان القرية لم
يلحظوا وجود القطة على الإطلاق.
ولكن توكوزو رأى أن إصابتها
خطيرة.

وقال لنفسه، "ربما أستطيع
إنقاذها." وعثر بسرعة على نزل
واصطحب القطة إلى داخله.

That night, Tokuzo stayed up late. He wrapped the cat's broken leg and made sure that the bed was warm and clean. "I'll name you 'Tama' – just like the round bell you are wearing," said Tokuzo.

وفي تلك الليلة، ظل توكوزو مستيقظاً حتى وقت متأخر. ولف قدم القطة المكسورة بالقماش وتأكد من أن الفراش دافئ ونظيف. وقال "سوف أسميك تاما' – مثل الجرس المستدير الذي حول عنقك.

The next morning, Tama opened its eyes and seemed to smile.

"Good, Tama. I am so relieved. Today is the big festival, but I'm going to stay behind in this small town with you instead. I want to be sure that you get well."

في الصباح التالي، فتحت تاما عينيها وبدا أنها تبتسم.

وقال توكوزو "هذا جيد يا تاما. أنا في غاية الارتياح. يوافق اليوم المهرجان الكبير، ولكنني سأظل في هذه المدينة الصغيرة معك بدلاً من ذلك. وأريد أن أتأكد من شفائك."

The following day, Tokuzo was able to sell a few toys to the village children. With the little money he earned, he bought two fish: one for himself, and one for Tama. "Tonight we'll celebrate!" he thought.

He returned to the inn and opened the door. "Tama…" he called. However, when he lit the candle, he discovered that Tama had died.

وفي اليوم التالي، استطاع توكوزو بيع عدد قليل من الألعاب لأطفال القرية. واشترى سمكتين بالنقود القليلة التي اكتسبها: واحدة لنفسه، والأخرى للقطة تاما. وقال لنفسه "سوف نحتفل الليلة!"

وعاد إلى النزل وفتح الباب، ثم نادى "تاما...". إلا أنه عندما أضاء الشمعة، اكتشف أن تاما قد ماتت.

The next morning, Tokuzo buried Tama in a grave overlooking the broad countryside. His heart was heavy with grief as he said goodbye.

وفي الصباح التالي، قام توكوزو بدفن تاما في قبر يطل على ريف فسيح. وكان قلبه مثقل بالأسى عند وداعها.

The big festival was almost over, but Tokuzo still had time. So he continued on his journey. Suddenly the sky grew dark. Rumbling thunder warned that a rainstorm was coming fast. He quickly ran to the closest tree for cover. The rain started to pour harder and harder.

كان المهرجان الكبير قد انتهى تقريباً، ولكن توكوزو كان لا يزال أمامه وقت. ولذا واصل رحلته. وفجأة أظلمت السماء. وكان صوت الرعد ينذر بقدوم عاصفة مطرية. وجرى بسرعة إلى أقرب شجرة ليختبئ تحتها. وزاد هطول المطر ازدياداً شديداً.

As Tokuzo wiped his face, he noticed a cat meowing by the temple gate. It seemed to be inviting him to come inside! Surprisingly, this cat looked like Tama, who had died just the day before.

وعندما مسح توكوزو وجهه، لاحظ قطة تموء بجانب بوابة المعبد. وقد بدا أنها تدعوه للدخول!
وللمفاجأة، كانت هذه القطة تشبه تاما، التي ماتت قبل يوم واحد فقط.

Tokuzo forgot about the rain. He ran toward the cat. "Tama, Tama… is that you? What are you doing here? I thought you died!" He had almost touched the cat, when suddenly…

ونسى توكوزو أمر المطر، وجرى نحو القطة. وقال "تاما، تاما... هل هذه أنت؟ ماذا تفعلين هنا؟ لقد اعتقدت أنك لقيت حتفك!" ولمس تقريباً القطة بيديه، وفجأة...

BAM! There was a huge explosion of light and sound. He turned around and gasped. The pine tree that had protected him from the rain had been split in half by a powerful bolt of lightning!

بووم! وكان هناك انفجار ضخم من الضوء والصوت. ونظر حوله لاهثا. وانقسمت شجرة الصنوبر
التي كانت تحميه من المطر إلى نصفين بسبب صاعقة برق قوية!

Tokuzo told everyone how a mysterious cat had saved him. The people were amazed at this story. They could not believe it. "How can cats know that lightning is going to strike? And if cats are dead, how can they call you?"

Tokuzo did not know how to answer. "I am sure that cat saved my life, but I have no way to prove it to you."

The *Osho-San* was listening carefully at the temple. "Maybe there is some truth here that we cannot explain. Tokuzo, please spend the night with us at the temple so that we can talk about it."

وأخبر توكوزو الجميع كيف أن قطة غامضة أنقذته. وكان الناس مندهشين من تلك القصة، ولم يصدقوها. "كيف تعرف القطط موعد البرق؟ وإذا كانت القطط ميتة، كيف يمكنها مناداتك؟" ولم يعرف توكوزو كيف يجيبهم. "أنا متأكد أن تلك القطة أنقذت حياتي، ولكن لا توجد لدي طريقة لأثبت ذلك. وكان أوشوسان ينصت باهتمام في المعبد. "ربما توجد هنا بعض الحقيقة التي لا نستطيع توضيحها. أرجو يا توكوزو أن تقضي معنا الليلة في المعبد حتى نستطيع الحديث عن ذلك."

He went to the meditation garden to think. "I was saved by Tama, and the people didn't believe it. What am I supposed to do next? I should create a statue of this cat," he thought, "so everybody can share my good luck."

He asked the *osho-san* for advice. "Let me introduce you to Old Master Craftsman. His daughter takes care of him because he is not well. But he is wise, and will tell you what you should do."

وذهب إلى حديقة التأمل للتفكير. وقال لنفسه "لقد أنقذتني تاما، ولكن الناس لا يصدقونني. ما الذي يفترض أن أقوم به بعد ذلك؟. يجب أن أصنع تمثالاً لتلك القطة بحيث يستطيع الجميع مشاركتي في الحظ الجيد."

وطلب النصيحة من أوشوسان. "اسمح لي أن أقدمك إلى الفنان الماهر الكبير في السن. إن ابنته تعتني به لأنه ليس بصحة جيدة. ولكنه حكيم وسوف يخبرك بما يجب عليك القيام به."

Old Master Craftsman was not feeling well, but he was happy to give Tokuzo some advice. "Clay is the best material for your statues, and my workshop has everything you will need. You are welcome to stay there. Unfortunately, you'll have to work by yourself, because I am too sick to help you."

لم يكن الفنان الماهر الطاعن في السن بصحة جيدة، ولكنه كان مسرورًا لتقديم بعض النصائح إلى توكوزو. "الصلصال هو أفضل مادة لتمثالك، وتحتوي ورشتي على كل شيء ستحتاجه. وأنا أرحب بإقامتك هناك. ولكن للأسف، سوف تعمل بنفسك لأنني مريض للغاية ولا أستطيع مساعدتك."

Tokuzo opened the workshop door. Where could he begin? Tools and supplies were everywhere! He felt lost, but at the same time very excited.

فتح توكوزو باب الورشة. وقال من أين ابدأ؟ وكانت الأدوات والمواد في كل مكان. وشعر بأنه تائه، ولكنه في الوقت ذاته كان يشعر بإثارة شديدة.

He started to follow Old
Master's directions. First, he had
to mix the clay.

وبدأ في اتباع توجيهات
الفنان الكبير.
أولاً، قام بمزج
الصلصال.

Then, he had to form it into the shape
of a cat. "These don't look like cats at all!"
he told himself.

بعد ذلك، كان عليه أن يقوم بتشكيله على شكل
قطة. وقال لنفسه، "إن هذه لا تبدو على شكل قطط
على الإطلاق."

Next, the clay had to be baked so
that it could harden. But to start a fire,
first wood had to be cut. This was much
more work than he had expected.

وبعد ذلك، كان لابد من تحميص
الصلصال بحيث يصبح صلباً. ولكن لإشعال النار،
كان لابد من قطع الأخشاب أولاً. وكان هذا العمل
أكثر بكثير من المتوقع.

Finally, the clay was baked! Tokuzo reached for the oven door, and peered down at his work. He couldn't believe his eyes. "Look at my cats! What did I do wrong?" His carefully formed statues had cracked and shattered into pieces.

وأخيراً، تم تحميص الصلصال! ووصل توكوزو إلى باب الفرن، وألقى نظرة على عمله.ولم يصدق عينيه. "انظر إلى قططي! ما الخطأ الذي فعلته؟ فقد تصدعت تماثيله المشكلة بعناية وتناثرت إلى قطع صغيرة.

He brought his work to Old Master Craftsman. "This can be a nice-looking cat, young man. But you did not mix the clay well, and the fire was too hot," he said.

Tokuzo would not give up. He needed more firewood, so he went back to the tree that had been struck by lightning. He started over again, and worked day and night.

وأحضر عمله إلى الفنان الماهر الكبير في السن الذي قال له، "من الممكن أن تكون هذه قطة جميلة الشكل، أيها الشاب. ولكنك لم تمزج الصلصال جيداً، وكانت النار حامية أكثر من اللازم."

ولكن توكوزو لم ييأس. واحتاج إلى المزيد من حطب الوقود، ولذا عاد إلى الشجرة التي ضربتها الصاعقة. وبدأ من جديد وعمل ليلا نهاراً.

One fine morning, Old Master was feeling a little better, and he came out to watch. He was impressed by Tokuzo's determination. "Your cats are looking much better. Now, why don't you make the arm swing by hiding a weight inside the body?" he asked. "The cleverest ideas are often hidden behind what the eye can see."

Tokuzo jumped up, amazed. "Yes! That will make the cat seem more alive. Thank you so much, *Sensei*!" Now Old Master started to get excited, too.

في صباح جميل، كان الفنان الكبير يشعر ببعض التحسن، وأتى للمشاهدة. وكان متأثراً من عزم توكوزو. وقال، "تبدو قططك أفضل بكثير." ثم سأل "والآن لماذا لا تجعل الذراع يتأرجح بإخفاء ثقل داخل الجسم؟ إن أفضل الأفكار هي غالباً تلك التي تكون خافية عن العين."

وقفز توكوزو مذهولاً، وقال "نعم! سوف أجعل تلك القطة تبدو أكثر حياة. أشكرك للغاية، سنسي!" وبدا الفنان الكبير يشعر بالإثارة هو الآخر.

A few weeks later, Tokuzo perfected
his cat. "Look, everyone! I did it! My
dream has finally come true!"
Old Master Craftsman came running from
his bed. "Good job! You did it!" he exclaimed.
His daughter was cheering, too. "How wonderful! My
father is running without his cane! Tokuzo, your cat has
chased his pain away!"

وبعد أسابيع قليلة، أتقن توكوزو تشكيل قطته. وقال "انظروا جميعاً! لقد
نجحت! لقد تحقق حلمي أخيراً!"

ونهض الفنان الماهر الكبير جرياً من فراشه، وصاح، "عمل جيد! لقد
نجحت!"

وكانت ابنته سعيدة أيضاً. وقالت، "رائع! إن أبي يجري دون عصاه! لقد
طردت قطتك آلامه!"

It happened that Old Master's daughter was a talented painter. So she helped decorate the statues. "This cat has a whole new life of its own!" Tokuzo was thrilled. They named the cat *Maneki Neko,* which means "The Cat That Invites Good Luck."

وللصدفة، كانت ابنة الفنان الماهر الكبير رسامة موهوبة. ولذا ساعدت في زخرفة التماثيل. وقال توكوزو وهو يشعر بالإثارة "لقد أصبح لهذه القطة حياة جديدة خاصة بها!" وأطلقوا على القطة اسم مانيكي نيكو ، الذي يعني "القطة التي تجلب الحظ الجيد."

Soon, *Maneki Neko* statues spread all over Japan, and everybody wanted to have one. As time passed, people started to say that a raised right paw brings fortune, and a raised left paw brings happiness and good luck.

وسرعان ما انتشرت تماثيل مانيكي نيكو في جميع أرجاء اليابان، وكان الجميع يرغب في الحصول على واحد. وبمرور الوقت، بدأ الناس يعتقدون بأن اليد اليمنى المرتفعة تجلب الحظ، وأن اليد اليسرى تجلب السعادة والحظ الجيد.

"*Osho-san*, did Tama really die?" Old Master asked.

"Well, the body can die, but the *kokoro* lives forever. Therefore, Tama can always remain in our hearts."

This story of the *Maneki Neko* reminds us that what we do is the cause of tomorrow. Even a tiny kitten might remember what we do. And it might even save our life. Or it might just be a friend forever and ever.

وسأل الفنان الكبير: "حضرة المحترم أوشو سان ، هل ماتت تاما حقاً ؟"

"حسناً، من الممكن أن يموت الجسد، ولكن كوكورو تعيش إلى الأبد. ولذا فإن تاما من الممكن أن تظل في القلوب إلى الأبد."

وتذكرنا قصة مانيكي نيكو هذه بما نقوم به من أجل الغد. بل وربما تذكرنا هرة صغيرة بما نقوم به. بل وربما تقوم بإنقاذ حياتنا. أو ربما تصبح صديقة للأبد.